See pocket on next page.

Singing Christmas carols and loving on the elderly at a local nursing home

Preparing a shoebox for Operation Christmas Child

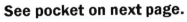

Walking for a cure

Delivering food to those in need in Mexico

## Grayslake Area Public Library District
### Grayslake, Illinois

1. A fine will be charged on each book which is not returned when it is due.

2. All injuries to books beyond reasonable wear and all losses shall be made good to the satisfaction of the Librarian.

3. Each borrower is held responsible for all books drawn on his card and for all fines accruing on the same.

**Amy Parker**
with illustrations by Daniel Fernández

Nashville, Tennessee

© 2013 by Amy Parker

Exclusive representation by Working Title Agency, LLC, Spring Hill, Tennessee

Published in 2013 by B&H Publishing Group, Nashville, Tennessee

ISBN: 978-1-4336-8084-7

Dewey Decimal Classification: JF

Subject Heading: CHRISTMAS—POETRY \ GENEROSITY—FICTION \ CHARITY—FICTION

Printed in China.

1 2 3 4 5 6 7 8 • 17 16 15 14 13

*My Christmas List*
is dedicated to Frederick,
who showed me what a Christmas list should be,
and to the children of Rwanda,
at the top of my list and in the bottom of my heart.

Dear God, this year I'm changing things—
Instead of toys and lots of stuff,
I want Christmas for the whole wide world,
Especially those without enough.

That little girl in Korea,
She only needs to hear Your name.
And a big, grown man in Russia,
Well, God, he just wants the same.

There are many kids in India
Without a place to live,
And a mom's sick in Uganda,
If there's a miracle to give.

Two brothers in Guatemala,
They're looking for water to drink.

(Um, and God, I'm sorry for
Letting mine go down the sink.)

A mom for the girl in China,
A daddy would be great, too,
And, Lord, that boy in Zambia,
He's running out of food.

Would You look down on the Sudan
And over in the Middle East?
They've been fighting for so long;
They could really use some peace.

And Christmas here on my street
Would be a job for Daniel's dad.

I heard his daddy telling mine,
It's the worst time they've ever had.

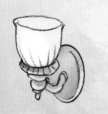

But dear God, more than anything—
What would help in every way—
Please help the whole wide world to know
Why You gave us Christmas Day.

Let them know that Your baby
Was a Savior for the earth;
Christmas for the world began
With this one baby's birth.

I know it's asking for a lot,
And I'll try to do my part. . . .

But this, God, is my Christmas list,
A list straight from my heart.

## Remember:

"Whatever you did for one of the least of these brothers of Mine, you did for Me." —Matthew 25:40

## Read:

Jesus tells the parable of the good Samaritan in Luke 10:25–37. He gives this as an example of how we should serve. No matter how different, how dirty, or how desperate others may appear, we are to be a neighbor to them all. As a kid, sometimes it can seem difficult to make a big difference, but watch for the people God sends your way. You may be surprised at how much of a difference those two little hands can make.

## Think:

1. Have you made your Christmas list this year? What are you asking for?

2. Why do you think the boy in the story is making a different kind of Christmas list this year?

3. How do you think he learned about those people in need?

4. What is he doing to be a neighbor to others?

5. Who do you know that needs a little help right now?

## Do:

Make your own Christmas list.

1. Get a piece of Christmassy paper or decorate your own.

2. Write "My Christmas List" at the top.

3. Make a list of at least five people or groups in your town or around the world who could use some help.

4. When you're finished, pray for each person or group on your list.

5. Talk to your parents or a church leader about helping them.

6. Hang the list on the fridge or a bathroom mirror, and pray for those people every time you see your list.

Ask God to show you people in need, at Christmas time and all year long.

Wrapping pj's for children in need

Showing our soldiers they are loved and appreciated by packing stockings for them

Befriending a needy child in Central America

Giving blankets, Bibles, and food to the homeless in our city